UREP
19/12

For Joyce and Kurt,
who always bring love —L.M.

For my sister, Miss Hannah Davies Junior,
who appears in this book —B.D.

Visit us on the Web!
randomhouse.com/kids

Educators and librarians, for a variety of teaching tools, visit us at
randomhouse.com/teachers

Library of Congress Cataloging-in-Publication Data
Moser, Lisa.
Railroad Hank / by Lisa Moser ; illustrations by Benji Davies. — 1st ed.
p. cm.
Summary: On his way to visit Granny Bett, who is feeling blue, Railroad Hank stops at the farms of several
friends and, misunderstanding their offers to help, winds up with a trainload of crazy cargo.
ISBN 978-0-375-86849-8 (trade) — ISBN 978-0-375-96849-5 (lib. bdg.)
[1. Railroad trains—Fiction. 2. Farm life—Fiction. 3. Humorous stories.] I. Davies, Benji, ill. II. Title.
PZ7.M84696Rai 2012 [E]—dc23 2011030231

MANUFACTURED IN CHINA
10 9 8 7 6 5 4 3 2 1
First Edition

Railroad Hank

by Lisa Moser

illustrated by Benji Davies

Random House 🏠 New York

Railroad Hank and his fine little train rolled down the track.

Railroad Hank stopped at Happy Flap Farm to talk with Missy May. "I'm headed up the mountain to see Granny Bett," said Railroad Hank. "She's feeling kind of blue."

"A plate of scrambley eggs always perks me up," said Missy May. "Take some of my eggs to Granny Bett."

Railroad Hank rubbed his chin. "But where do you get eggs?"
"From my hens, of course," said Missy May.

"Okey dokey," said Railroad Hank.

HAPPY FLAP FARM
EGGS FOR SALE!
(BY THE DOZEN)

"Wait!" yelled Missy May.
"Take the eggs! Not the hens!"

Railroad Hank stopped at Dandelion Dairy to talk with Country Carl. "I'm headed up the mountain to see Granny Bett," said Railroad Hank. "She's feeling kind of blue."

"A glass of creamy milk always makes me feel better," said Country Carl. "Take some of my milk to Granny Bett."

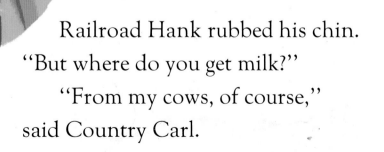

Railroad Hank rubbed his chin. "But where do you get milk?"

"From my cows, of course," said Country Carl.

"Okey dokey," said Railroad Hank.

"Wait!" yelled Country Carl.
"Take the milk! Not the cows!"

Chugga Chugga, Chugga Chugga, WOO WOO WOO!!

Railroad Hank stopped at Fish-Jump Pond to talk with Reel-'Em-In Sam. "I'm headed up the mountain to see Granny Bett," said Railroad Hank. "She's feeling kind of blue."

"A sizzling pan of fresh fish always tickles my toes," said Reel-'Em-In Sam. "Take some of my fish to Granny Bett."

Railroad Hank rubbed his chin. "But where do you get fish?"

"From my pond, of course," said Reel-'Em-In Sam.

"Okey dokey," said Railroad Hank.

"Wait!" yelled Reel-'Em-In Sam.
"Take the fish! Not the pond!"

Railroad Hank stopped at Applesauce Hill to talk with Cinnamon Cobbler. "I'm headed up the mountain to see Granny Bett," said Railroad Hank. "She's feeling kind of blue."

"A crunchy red apple always sweetens my day," said Cinnamon Cobbler. "Take some of my apples to Granny Bett."

Railroad Hank rubbed his chin.
"But where do you get apples?"
"From my trees, of course,"
said Cinnamon Cobbler.

"Okey dokey," said Railroad Hank.
"Wait!" yelled Cinnamon Cobbler.
"Take the apples! Not the tree!"

Railroad Hank chugged up and up the mountain
to see Granny Bett.

"We heard you were feeling blue, and everyone
sent something to help," said Railroad Hank.

He threw open the train doors one by one.
Chickens squawked. Cows stampeded. Water
sloshed, and apples rolled.

Granny Bett looked at all the chaos.
She hooted and snorted and slapped her leg.
She shook until her bonnet slid sideways
and her shoelaces popped.

"Granny Bett!" cried Railroad Hank.
"Are you still blue?"

"Oh no," said Granny Bett, giggling.
"I'm right dandy."

"What fixed you?" asked Railroad Hank.
"Was it the eggs or the milk or the fish or the apples?"

"It was you," said Granny Bett. "And all the friends you brought to visit. Now let's have a friend-celebrating, glad-you-came, I'm-all-better-now kind of day!"

"Okey dokey!" cheered Railroad Hank, and he threw his hat in the air.

As the sun set, Railroad Hank helped everyone find
a seat on his fine little train.

"That was a wonderful surprise!" said Granny Bett.
"Now I'm just going to sit and relax and dream about all
the fun we had."

Railroad Hank rubbed his chin. "But where do you
sit and relax?"

"On my porch swing, of course," said Granny Bett.

"Okey dokey," said Railroad Hank.